Curse-Proof!

Eric B. Hare

Pacific Press® Publishing Association
Nampa, Idaho
Oshawa, Ontario, Canada
www.pacificpress.com

Cover design by Lars Justinen
Cover art by Lars Justinen
Inside design by Steve Lanto

Additional copies of this book are available by
calling toll free 1-800-765-6955
or by visiting http://www.adventistbookcenter.com.

ISBN 13: 978-0-8163-2208-4
ISBN 10: 0-8163-2208-2

07 08 09 10 11 · 5 4 3 2 1

Dedication

To Yea Mwe (Perfume),

Known and loved by three generations of Hares!

Contents

The Three Brothers

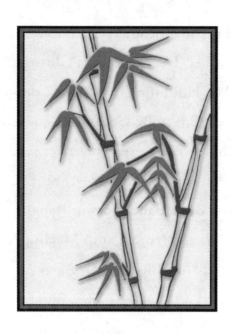

Chapter 1

I can see them now, three brothers standing timidly in my office with their father, who had brought them to school. I wrote their names down in the register: Maung Thein, fourteen years old; Aung Thein, ten; and Aung Twe, nine. I was still musing on their names, which meant "Mr. Victor," "Conquering Victor," and "Conquering Dog," when their father spat a mouthful of betel nut juice out of the window and asked, "What are the school fees, Thara?"

"Twenty rupees each," I replied. "That will make sixty rupees for the three, Uncle."

"Fine," he said, and putting his hand into the big bag he carried on his shoulder, he produced sixty solid silver rupees and placed them on my desk.

My eyes glistened, and I said to myself, "Good stuff!" You know, I like cash in advance, don't you? It's good business, and I like it.

"And how much do you estimate their books and clothes will cost for the year, Thara?" again asked the father. Now I can estimate very well under such circumstances, and it didn't take me long to say, "About forty-five rupees, Uncle."

"Fine," he said, and into that same bag went his hand again, and he produced forty-five more solid silver rupees and put them on my table. And once more I said to myself, "Good stuff!" And I marked, "Paid in advance" by the names of the three brothers and decided to follow their progress closely. They were good-looking lads. The father was a good-looking man. Almost at once I could feel myself expecting more of them than of the average students. They had paid cash in advance. They meant business.

The mission school was a new and different experience for them. The regular program, the work, the classes, the silent study hours, the daily drill, the singing, the brass band—how different it all was from the irregular, noisy, monotonous singing of the Buddhist temple, the only school they had ever known. They put their whole heart and soul into everything; and when the first vacation came, what wonderful stories they took home to their village! They had learned some words of the white man's language, and the village children clapped their hands with delight when they said, "What-is-your-name?" "Where-do-you-live?" "What-are-you-doing?" The two younger boys told of the bricks they had made in the brick-making class, and the big boy, Maung Thein, who had been in the building class, demonstrated his skill by making his father a chair.

A chair! The village folk could hardly imagine such a thing. Maung Thein, who had never handled a plane or a saw or a hammer before, had made his father a chair! And they crowded around to admire that chair and to pat it and to stroke it. And if there was one thing that Father loved doing more than anything else, it was to sit in that chair.

The boys came to school for the second year. Again they paid cash in advance and worked and studied as if they intended to get their money's worth out of their education. During the second vacation, Maung Thein made his father a table. A table! And again the village folk gathered around to admire the table and to stroke it and pat it. And if there was anything that Father loved doing more than sitting in the chair his son had made, it was to sit in the chair near the table.

"Maung Thein, my son," he said one day, "you have done very well at school. Very well! I am getting old, and someday I will be too old to be the village chief anymore. Then I want to make you the village chief in my place. I dream of it every day. There is only one thing, my son, listen to me carefully. Beware of the white man's religion. Have nothing to do with it. Nothing. We are spirit worshipers, and as slaves of the devils we cannot walk in the ways of the white man's God." He paused and looked into Maung Thein's face to see what he would say.

But he answered not a word. Was his face flushed just a little?

"Father, I Want to Be a Christian"

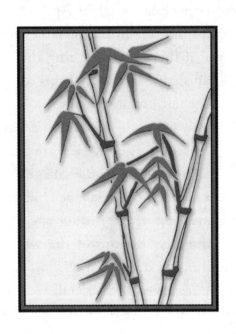

Chapter 2

For the third year the boys came back to school, and it was another good year for them. In addition to the usual work and study program, Maung Thein was asked to play the trombone in the brass band. The younger brothers danced with delight as they saw their older brother push and pull and make beautiful music with his slide trombone.

During the year, the father and mother came up to visit the school one day, and the boys proudly showed them around the mission compound. As I was coming back to the mission house after treating a patient in the dispensary, I overheard Maung Thein saying as he and his father and his mother stood looking at the new boys' dormitory, "This is *our* house. *We* built it. The two little fellows helped to make the bricks, and I was one of the carpenters." And his chest stuck out with legitimate pride as they stood for a moment examining the beautiful building. And once more I said to myself, "Good stuff!" You know, I like to hear boys and girls talking about "*our* school" and "*our* message" and "*our* work." It puts the right vision into their hearts. They are "*our* mission-aries" and "*our* preachers" and "*our* boys." It's good business, being coworkers and partners together with God, and I like it.

It was not long after this, however, that the parents began to worry. Their happiness gave way to perplexity as the boys showed their unwillingness to take part in the devil feasts and to join in the worship of the yellow-robed Buddhist priests. And their fear soon turned to anger when after four years of school Maung Thein came home for the summer vacation and said, "Father, I want to be baptized. I want to become a Christian."

"Get baptized, huh?" the angry parents raged. "That's not what we sent you to school for. Baptized! Huh! The idea! What shame we would have to bear!"

"But Father, if you only under—"

"Understand? If you want to get baptized, I'll baptize you myself," shouted the angry father. "Next year you shall stay home from school and plant rice with me, and I'll baptize your arms and your legs in mud! That's the kind of baptism you need!"

It was only after much promising and pleading that a compromise was reached, and Maung Thein came back to school alone. "I've promised my mother and father that I won't be baptized this year, Thara," he said. "It was the only way I could get back to school. But I can keep coming to the Little Brothers' class [the baptismal class], can't I?"

"You surely can, Maung Thein," I encouraged, "and who can tell, maybe God will change your parents' hearts.

You be sure to pray for them and live up to all the light you have. I will pray too, and be assured the Spirit of God will tell you very definitely just when you should be baptized."

The year went by. Maung Thein had to work his way through school that year. His father had refused to pay any fees for him. Though often discouraged at the anger of his parents, Maung Thein was happy that he could suffer for Christ, and he prayed and prayed earnestly that the Spirit of God would change his parents' hearts. At last the camp meeting of the new year drew near, and the father and mother came up to visit again. But the light had gone out of their faces, and only the dark anger of evil spirits was visible there.

"Won't you have a talk with Father and Mother, Thara?" Maung Thein pleaded. That night we invited them to our home. We had some music on the phonograph, a little refreshment, and talked pleasantly enough about rice and bullocks. Then I said, "Uncle, I would like to talk to you about Maung Thein," and the atmosphere changed at once. "You know," I said, "Maung Thein is a good lad, and God is moving on his heart to become a Christian."

Have you ever been in a cave and put out your light and felt the darkness? The darkness seems so dense that you can feel it with your fingers. In the same way, you can feel the presence of evil spirits. And this evening I was conscious that these poor people were surrounded by evil angels. My words seemed to go no further than my lips. They made no sign that they either heard or understood, and after a moment, without a word, they turned their backs and left our house. Nor did they speak a word to anyone else or partake of a parting meal, but left sullenly and angrily for their home in the darkness of the night.

"I wonder what they will do next, Maung Thein?" I whispered.

"I do not know," Maung Thein replied fearfully. "I wonder!"

"We Hold the Devil Feast Tonight"

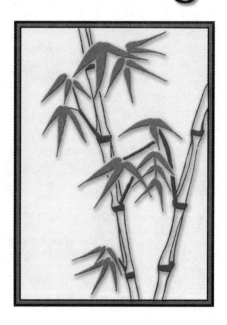

Chapter 3

In a few more weeks the camp meeting started, and on the Friday evening when the call was made for those to stand who wanted to be baptized, Maung Thein stood among the first.

"You know, your father has not given his permission for you to baptized yet, Maung Thein," I said as I came to him during the examination of the candidates. "And though you have waited the year according to your promise, it will likely mean that you will have to stand alone. Do you feel, Maung Thein, that you can stand alone?"

"No, Thara, I don't," was his quick reply. "I am very weak, but the Savior I have found here at school is very strong. He has promised to be with me always. If Paul could do all things through Christ, cannot I? I am of age now. According to the law of the land, I can make my own decisions. I may be disowned and cut off from my inheritance, but I am going to follow my Savior come what may."

Who can withhold water that such a young man, with such faith in his Savior, should not be baptized?

So the next day, among the other precious candidates, Maung Thein was baptized. It was a happy day for us. We stood there on the river bank singing "Happy Day," but away down in Maung Thein's village the powers of darkness were at work, and the next morning at six o'clock a messenger arrived looking for Maung Thein. Finding him, he spat furiously onto the ground and between clenched teeth hissed the word "dog!" Then he threw a folded piece of paper on the ground in front of him.

Maung Thein trembled, then stooped to pick up the note. As he read, his face paled; his heart thumped hard; and the cold perspiration broke out all over his face. He turned away from the man who had brought the note and went quickly to the mission house and knocked on the door.

The door was opened by a beautiful maiden who bore the lovely character name of Yea Mwe, meaning "perfume." She was helping us in our home duties so that Mrs. Hare could give all of her time to the mission work.

"Maung Thein!" she said in surprise as she saw his troubled face. "What brings you here so early in the morning. Are you in trouble?"

"Yes," he said weakly. "I must see Thara."

"They are sitting at the table eating breakfast," she said, "but I am sure Thara will talk to you. If you are in trouble, Thara would rather help you than eat."

I heard them talking at the door and rose at once to see what the matter was. As soon as I saw Maung Thein's pale face, I knew something was wrong. "Tell me, Maung Thein," I said, "what is the matter?"

He unfolded the note the messenger had just brought, placed it in my hand, and said, "Thara, please read this."

And I read,

"We hold the devil feast tonight.

We require your presence with us.

Your Father."

"What shall I do now, Thara?" he asked. "I cannot partake of the devil feast anymore. I am a Christian now." Nobody could eat. The whole household was standing around trying to take in the situation.

"Don't you give up whatever you do," Perfume said. "I had an experience something like that too."

"You did?" Maung Thein said unbelievingly.

"Yes," Perfume continued. "My folks called me a Jew and a dog and a seventh-day female."

"Oh," Maung Thein said sympathetically. "I thought by your happy face that you had always been a Seventh-day Adventist."

"Indeed no. Sometime I'll tell you about it. But just keep faithful whatever you do. God will help you somehow."

"Yes, I am sure God will help you some way," I assured him, "but for the time being, write Father a nice letter and tell him that you love him more than ever now that you are a Christian, and tell him that he will be proud of you some day." He wrote a letter that would soften the heart of almost any parent, but it had no effect on the enraged father in the village. And the next day there arrived two messengers. One said, "Maung Thein, your mother has gone crazy. She has to be watched continually lest she hang herself." The other messenger handed him another note from his father, and again Maung Thein's face went pale as he read,

"This baptism cannot be.

It must be undone,

It must be turned inside out and dismantled.

We hold the devil feast tonight.

You must be here."

"It's Got to Be Undone"

Chapter 4

"What will I do now, Thara?" Maung Thein whispered as he stood there trembling with the letter in his hand.

"Let us go over and talk with Brother Baird," I said. Brother Harold Baird was my associate missionary. He also was a graduate nurse and a very skilled practical man. It was his skill that had gradually turned our leaf and bamboo school buildings into beautiful permanent wood buildings, and his counsel and advice were always eagerly sought.

"What do you think of that?" I asked after he had read the letter.

"Of course Maung Thein must go," he said slowly.

"But he must not go alone," I added.

"No, not alone. I will be glad to go with him if you think it best," he said at last.

The news soon spread around, and we all went down to the launch landing to see them off, for Maung Thein's village was just twenty miles downriver and then three miles inland from the riverbank.

"Goodbye, and God bless you," we chorused. And Perfume added, "Don't give up whatever you do."

It took only three hours to make the journey, and as they came to the clearing that surrounded the village, Maung Thein whispered, "Here we are. And that's my house over there. See where those two big boys are? They are my brothers."

"I wonder why they are not out in the field at work," Brother Baird said.

"Yes, I wonder, too," Maung Thein whispered.

As they neared the house, the two brothers saw them and called, "He's come! Maung Thein's come!" Immediately the whole family emerged from the doorway of the bamboo house and stood looking at them from the verandah. The next second, the figure of a little woman with a rope in her hand sprang from the verandah and ran screaming into the forest.

"Look, look, it's Mother," the two sisters screamed as they also sprang from the verandah and gave chase. "She's going into the jungle to hang herself!" They stopped only long enough to give a hateful, withering look at Maung Thein and to say, "It's all your fault. It's all your fault. You've driven your mother mad, and if she commits suicide, we'll call you a murderer!"

Meanwhile, in response to the shouting, the village crowd gathered and began to chorus suggestions: "Why don't you undo it? Why don't you undo this baptism?" And as the two sisters came back with the angry, screaming mother, the village witch arrived on the scene. Yes, a real witch, a woman who communed with evil spirits and had power to bewitch and cast spells of magic. She was greatly feared and respected by all the villagers. As her shrill voice rose above the noise, the crowd quieted down and listened to hear what she would have to say.

"Don't you remember," she shrieked, "once before when one of our villagers was baptized and became a God-worshiper, that same night a tiger came into our village and ate one of his family?"

"Yes, yes, we remember," the crowd cried.

"That's just what will happen again this time. I tell you, it's got to be undone. This baptism's got to be undone! May the curse of Moo-Kaw-Lee, the evil one, haunt him day and night and give him bad, horrible dreams," she screamed. And the crowd joined in an ever-swelling chant: "It's got to be undone. It's got to be undone. It's got to be undone."

In vain Brother Baird and Maung Thein tried to explain, but the frenzied crowd would not listen. And it looked as if there were only a step between them and being torn to pieces by the threatening mob.

"Well, we will take your message back to the big Thara," they shouted, "and we will see what he will say."

"Aye, aye," yelled the crowd. And Maung Thein's father added, "In three days we will hold the devil feast. You must be here with all this baptism business undone—dead or alive."

That evening, as we heard the motor launch chugging its way back up the river, an anxious group of students and teachers gathered down at the landing.

"Now what am I going to do, Thara?" Maung Thein said as he told of the terrifying experience he had just been through.

I replied, "Maung Thein, we have three days. Remember you are curse-proof. I'm going to pray and fast for three days. Then we will see what God will do."

"I will pray and fast, too," he said.

"I will, too," Perfume said.

"I will, too," each of the teachers said.

"So will we; so will we," the students chorused.

The Seventh-day Female

Chapter 5

I know how you feel, Maung Thein," Perfume whispered as they walked up to the mission house from the boat landing.

"You do?" Maung Thein questioned.

"Yes, let me tell you," Perfume said. "You see, my folks were not heathens. They were Christians of another church. But my father had passed away, and it was kind of hard for Mother to keep the family fed and clothed, so when I heard that Thara and Ma Ma Hare needed someone to help with the housework, I was very happy to come. When I left home, my friends said, 'Now be careful of those seventh-day people. They are Jews, and they will make you sacrifice and eat the Passover.' "

"Sacrifice and eat the Passover?" Maung Thein said unbelievingly.

"Yes, but I told them nobody would ever make me into a Jew. I had bought a new Bible, and I would show them. Well to my great joy, I found everybody just lovely here at the mission. They gave me my Sundays off, and they didn't make me go to church on Sabbath. I even cooked pork stew to eat with my rice occasionally. And it was the school children who told me first. They said, 'Oh, who wants to eat pork? Don't you know the Bible says it's unclean?' and they showed me the Bible text, and I marked it. Then I said, 'But that was only for the Jews,' and they said, 'Noah wasn't a Jew, and God told him about unclean animals nearly a thousand years before there was a Jew!' So I marked all the texts, and I thought, *I must show my folks at home these things.* 'How glad they will be to know,' I said."

"This is getting interesting," Maung Thein said. "Let's sit down while you tell me the rest."

"Well I found out the seventh-day people were not Jews and didn't sacrifice or eat the Passover. I began to go to Sabbath School. Their worship was just like ours. They sang the same songs, and I marked every verse in my new Bible. But I kept on keeping my Sunday. I said, 'They will never make me a Seventh-day believer.' Then I went home for three weeks in the summer. I took my marked Bible with me. At first my folks at home were glad to see how well I looked. I said, 'It's because I don't eat pork or prawns or unclean foods anymore,' and I showed them the verses in my Bible. But they looked at me, and they said, 'You're mad! You're a Jew. You're a seventh-day female!' "

"A seventh-day female? And you were still keeping Sunday!" Maung Thein said in amazement.

"Yes, and all the time I was home they cooked nothing but prawns and pork to eat with our rice. I nearly starved because I ate only salt with my rice, and even when I left, they tilted their noses in the air and said, 'Huh! This seventh-day female thinks she can teach us. We'll get the pastor to straighten her out.' "

"Perfume, I'm proud of you," Maung Thein breathed. "You sure do know how I feel just now."

"Yes, and when I got back to the mission, I wrote to my Sunday pastor and asked him for the texts to straighten me out. But the texts never came, and I found everything the seventh-day people taught was in the Bible. I soon stopped keeping Sunday, and I was baptized. Then next summer I went home, and I said, 'Now you can call me a seventh-day female all you like, for I've been baptized. Go and call the pastor. I'll call all my friends, and let us have a meeting.' But the pastor was away, and my friends were too busy, and so . . .'"

"Perfume! Perfume! You were just a young woman, and you were all alone. And yet you were not afraid! Perfume, I think you are wonderful!"

"And I think you are, too," said Perfume. Then she suddenly realized she had work to do, so she jumped up quickly and ran into the house. There was a happiness in her heart and a flush on her cheek, and she found herself singing as she went about her work.

And strangely, Maung Thein's heart was lighter, too, as he went on his way. "She is going to pray for me," he said to himself. "So are Thara and all the teachers. And all the students and everybody have decided to have only one meal a day for three days. God will—He surely will—He'll change my parents' hearts or He'll give me courage to attend the devil feast alone."

"You Are No Longer My Son"

Chapter 6

It seemed clear to us all, as we prayed and fasted, that Thara Peter, our evangelist, and I should go to visit with Maung Thein's parents on the morning of the third day and leave Maung Thein at the school until we could feel out their attitude. So, calling one of the big boys for added company, we went down the river by launch and were soon approaching Maung Thein's village. "Oh God, send a company of angels with us to drive back the powers of darkness," we prayed as we bowed with our heads together, and God did.

"Hello, Uncle," I called out as cheerfully as I could as I went up into the house and found the father and the mother alone.

"Uh," Maung Thein's father grunted in surprise. "Oh, it's Thara! Are there just three of you?" for at a glance he could see that Maung Thein was not with us.

"Oh, no, Uncle," I replied. "There are a whole lot of us. You can see only three of us. The others are angels, and we have come to cheer you up; the angels will keep the evil spirits away and give you peace of heart."

"But where is Maung Thein?" he asked.

"He stayed behind," I replied.

And the mother, who up to this point had been sitting sullenly on the floor sifting rice, now sat motionless. God was with us. It didn't just happen that most of the villagers were away at their work. There was no furious crowd. There was no screaming witch. And God gave us words. While I talked, Peter prayed. Then Peter talked, and I prayed. We told them of the love of God, of His wonderful ways in finding out honest ones who were worshiping God as well as they knew how. We reminded the father of the wonderful way he had been led to bring his boys to the mission school, of the things the boys had learned, and we pleaded with him to acknowledge this God who was so anxious to lead them all the way.

The father was moved. It was hard for him to speak. But at last he said, "Well, anyway, to keep up appearances I will cut off his support and cut off his inheritance, and if he wants to keep on worshiping God, he will have to work his own way through school."

We were glad enough to hear even a statement like that. Then after the father had spoken, the mother coughed and cleared her throat. She neither looked at us nor spoke to us, but opening her mouth she prayed and cursed, and cursed and prayed, as only a heathen mother could do:

"God of the heaven
God of the earth,
Today is the full of the moon.

Today you will visit the earth.
You will walk among the cocoanut palms;
You will walk among the banana trees;
You will see me in my sorrow;
You will see me in my tears,
because my son is dead,
because my son is no more.
Whereas before I had nine children,
now I have only eight
for one is gone to heaven,
but he won't go the same path with us.
No longer is he my son;
no longer am I his mother.
May the curse of Moo-Kaw-Lee, the evil one,
haunt him day and night
and give him bad, horrible dreams until he dies.
When I hear he is rotting in the grave
and the worms have eaten out his eyes,
may I not be moved to pity
and call him again my son.
When he hears that I am rotting in my grave
and worms have eaten my eyes out,
let him not return to call me Mother."

There is no bitterness greater than hopeless, heathen bitterness. There are no curses more awful than the despairing curses of those who know not the love of God.

We rose to our feet, commended the parents to the love of Christ, and assured them that we would be praying every day that God would reveal His love to them and give them hope and peace.

Then we brought the news back to Maung Thein. "Your parents acknowledge your baptism, but have cast you off as their son."

"What shall I do now?" Maung Thein said.

"My lad," I replied, "we have all done all we can do. Now we must wait upon the Lord to see what He will do."

"Will God take away the anger from my parents' hearts sometime, Thara?"

"I think He will, Maung Thein. I think He will," I assured him. "Remember, you are curse-proof."

And God did! How do you think He did it?

The Brass Band
Goes to Rangoon

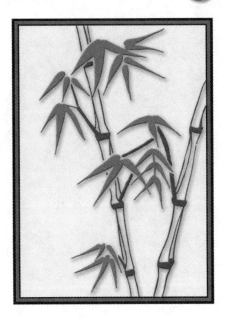

Chapter 7

The next three weeks on the mission station were filled with excitement. School was over; the camp meeting was over; and the next big event was that our Jungle Brass Band was going to Rangoon city to give a program in connection with the Ingathering campaign. Elder George Pettit, pastor of the Rangoon church, had finally obtained committee sanction for the trip. It was almost more than we could believe. Of the twenty-four boys in the school, only two or three had ever ridden on a train. And now all the band was going downriver to Moulmein on the riverboat, then all night on the train to Rangoon! Each boy had been given a pair of black shiny trousers, a white shirt bought in the Moulmein bazaar, and a cork helmet. How marvelous they looked! The instruments had all been run through the repair shop. We had fitted two new drum heads, put in six new valve springs, fixed four water keys, straightened out two dented bells, soldered two cracked seams, and made four lyres. Recreation time saw little else but brass polish and practice.

The news that the jungle boys were to ride the river steamer and the fire cart (the railway train) and were going to the white man's city where the streets were paved and the motorcars and the lightning cars (the streetcars) went up and down the streets spread rapidly around the district.

Now, as you know, Maung Thein played one of the slide trombones in the jungle band, and little by little the news reached his village where his mother and father were still feeling upset and angry over Maung Thein's baptism. And the women of the village came to Maung Thein's mother and said, "So your son is going to the big city! And he will see the fire cart and the lightning cart, and ride on the fire boat, and see the animals in the zoo, and see the great fire boats that cross the ocean! He will come back, seeing more in just a few days than we have seen in all our lives. We wish *our* sons played in the band. We wish *our* sons could go to the white man's city."

Of course, she wouldn't admit it, but Maung Thein's mother smiled in spite of herself and straightened up her head as she thought of all the honor her son was bringing upon the family.

At last the day came. The Jungle Band went by mission launch to Shwegon, twenty miles away, and boarded the river steamer for Moulmein. The excitement of the boys and the excitement of the passengers as they admired the band boys in their lovely uniforms with their beautiful shining instruments was reward enough for the work and preparation that had gone into this trip.

At last the whistle blew, the bell clanged, the gang-plank was pulled up, and we were off! Slowly down the river, past beautiful mountains and vast paddy lands we went, stopping at the villages on both sides of the river to take on and let off passengers and freight. Was it the third village? I noticed a little old lady with two strong boys beside her. I tried to see her face, but it was covered with her hands. She was sitting apart from the passengers that were coming and going, and I would have thought no more of it, but as the steamer started off again, Maung Thein came bounding into my cabin.

"Did you see her, Thara? Did you see her?" he asked excitedly, his voice choked with emotion.

"See whom?" I asked.

"Mother and Aung Thein and Aung Twe," he replied.

"Was that little lady your mother?"

"Yes, Thara, it was my mother! As the boat stopped I saw her at once, and I knew it was her! I saw her looking at the brass instruments stacked in a neat pile; then I saw her look from one band boy to another till she saw me. Her face lit up, and I saw her say, 'My son.' Then she began to cry and covered her face with her hands. But Thara, she called me 'My son'! God's doing it; God's doing it! He's softening their hearts. Oh, I'm so glad!"

And you should have heard that trombone play in Rangoon city! Some of the boys got sick that night on the train. One boy lost his ticket. Two boys came down with malaria, but the next morning at six-thirty we marched to the mission house and went into the back room of the church, where we slept, and ate, and rested, and washed and pressed our uniforms, and got ready for the program that night.

More than three hundred people filled the outdoor garden beside the church. The Lord Mayor of Rangoon was chairman for the occasion. As soon as he was seated, the Jungle Brass Band marched to the platform, and the program went off without a hitch. The applause was tremendous. The Lord Mayor's speech was very flattering, and the collection for Ingathering that night amounted to 177 rupees.

But you should have heard Maung Thein's trombone. He seemed to have new life that night, and his old trombone seemed to be saying all the time, "He's doing it; He's doing it. God is changing my parents' hearts. I wonder what *He* will do next."

At the Awbawa Camp Meeting

Chapter 8

"Maung Thein, what did you like the very best in all the big city?" Ohn Bwint asked as they sat in the train on the way to the Awbawa camp meeting just two days after the wonderful Ingathering program. Ohn Bwint played the tuba in the band, and he was always the center of attention because he had the biggest instrument of all.

"It's hard to tell," Maung Thein replied. "The wide streets, the motorcars—maybe the lift [elevator] in the great big shop. What did you like best?"

"Oh, I liked everything, too," Ohn Bwint said, "but when I saw those great big boats that go over the ocean, I couldn't believe my eyes. They are like a city on the water, and if it was a mother boat, it could have a very large family of river boats like the one we ride on going to Shwegon."

"Yes, and the animals . . . "

"I'm sure glad I'm in the band, aren't you? And we didn't make any mistakes!"

"My trombone played better than it ever did before," Maung Thein said. "I think it must have been happy because my mother came to see me at the riverside and called me 'my son' again."

"We were all happy, Maung Thein," Ohn Bwint said quietly. Then he added, "You know, I have been cast out and disowned, too."

"You have?"

"Yes, I wanted to be baptized three years ago, but my parents got very angry and threatened to disown me; I couldn't stand to think of it. So I promised them I would wait. Then when the camp meeting came, and the other boys in the baptismal class were baptized, I was the most unhappy boy in the world. I sat under a bush all by myself, and when the first boy was baptized, it just seemed to me I could see Jesus standing before His Father, and I could almost hear Him say, 'He's Mine, Father. See, Father, here are the nail prints. I paid the price for him. He's not afraid to confess Me before men. I'm not ashamed to confess him before Thee. And this one coming down into the water now, Father, he's Mine, and the next one, too, Father, and the next one, too. But Father, not that one over there under the bush. He's afraid to be disowned. He's even afraid his father will tell the devils that he's dead. He's not Mine, Father.' And oh, Maung Thein, I couldn't stand it. To think that Christ loved me so much and suffered for me so much, and I was afraid to be disowned. So I went home again and told my parents that whether they disowned me or not, I would have to be baptized. Of course they were angry and disappointed, but as the months and years have gone by, they are not angry anymore."

"Maybe someday my parents won't be angry anymore either," Maung Thein said hopefully.

The camp meeting at the outstation of Awbawa was a grand success. The meeting had been well advertised, and people came from far and near. One old uncle stood near Maung Thein with his eyes bugging out, watching him push and pull as he played his trombone. When the band stopped for breath, he looked closely at Maung Thein and asked, "How do you swallow that thing in and out without straightening out your neck?"

Maung Thein smiled and showed him how the slide worked and said, "Do you like the band?"

"Like it?" he said. "Of course I like it, but I was awfully scared of it at first. When I got to the village, everybody was talking about the band, and I said, 'Where is it?' And they said, 'Down there near the school. Come on, and we'll take you.' But I said, 'Nothing doing. It'll see me. Wait till it's dark.' They laughed and said, 'It won't eat you.' But I said, 'Never mind; I don't want to get too close to it.' So I sneaked around the back of the village and came in gradually behind it. I saw three people under a paddy barn that was about three feet off the ground, so I sneaked under the barn with them, and there I could see it all. Twenty-one of them in black trousers and white shirts with shining brass horns! There were big ones and little ones, fat ones and thin ones, and pulling in and out ones. I sure did think you swallowed it. And I was not the only one who was scared. I saw some folks behind a fence. There were half a dozen in a wood pile, and behind every tree there were as many as there could be.

"Well, just then the white Thara said something, and all those boys got very quiet and looked serious. Me, too. I held my breath! Then that white man's hand moved up and down once or twice, and that whole thing started—the big ones, the little ones, the pulling-in-and-out ones, the drums, and everything. They were all playing different, yet it was all together just the same, and nobody could move till the band stopped for breath. I couldn't even chew my wad of betel nut. I didn't even know it had rolled out of my mouth till the band stopped. Then I knew that I'd lost it. After a while they started off again, and ah, me, it was lovely! And every time they played I felt it was nicer and nicer. I didn't want them to stop. I didn't want to go home anymore. I didn't want to eat rice anymore, and I just came up closer and closer. They say none of the band boys chew betel nut. Is that so?"

"That's right. None of us chews betel nut or smokes either," Maung Thein said.

"They say that all of the band boys are God-worshipers. Is that so?"

"That's right; all of the boys are Christians."

"What is a Christian?"

"Listen, the big Thara is going to tell you now. Listen!"

Over the Hills and Far Away

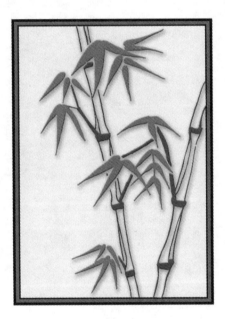

Chapter 9

The white Thara stood up in the middle of the brass band with the crowd of happy villagers all around. Of course, you know that I was the white Thara. I told them a simple little story to illustrate God's love.

Once when I was a very little boy, a dog bit me, and ever after that I didn't like dogs and never had one in my home. But one day my little boy brought home a little black dog. At first, I said he couldn't keep it and that we would look for a home for it and give it away. But when I saw how much my little boy loved that dog—how he shared his dinner with it and his milk with it and sometimes took it to bed with him—I said, "All right then, although I don't like dogs, I'll let you keep him because you love him so much." And we wouldn't give that dog away, and we wouldn't sell him for any price. That's the way it is with God and us. We were sinners and had no right to a home in heaven. But Jesus, the Son of God, loves us and came to earth and shared our food with us and our homes with us, and He loved us so much that God said, "All right, I'll give a home in heaven to every

51

man and woman and child who will show that they love You by obeying You."

"Ah, ah, ah!" the village folks chorused. "That's the way it is. And that's why all the band boys are Christians."

The next day we had three meetings, and the next day three more. Then we decided to walk back to the mission station, about 120 miles over the hills and through the valleys, and preach the gospel with the band in every village on the way. It was a wonderful trip. The boys were wonderful. We started about three o'clock every morning so we could march about twelve or twenty miles before the heat of the day. Then after a little rest, we would visit and treat the sick. And about five o'clock in the evening we would start up the band. The village people loved it. They had never heard of anything like it, and the clean, happy boys left a hunger in the heart of many a village boy to attend a mission school. All went well until about the fifth day. Then as we left the chief's house in the village of Tasuder, he said, "There's a good clear trail over the hills to Lerdo-Ki, Thara, but look out for tigers."

"Tigers! Tigers!" I heard the boys whispering to each other.

"Yes, tigers. Six of them. The last people who came over the hill a few days ago said they saw them. But if you'll play the band for them, they won't hurt you, I'm sure."

"We're not scared of tigers; we'll play the band to them," the boys said smilingly, and we started off.

A few miles along the trail we came to another village close to the path. The people had come to our meeting the night before, but now branches were put across the entrance to the village, and branches were hung on the bamboo ladders.

"That means there is sickness over on the other side of the mountain," Ohn Bwint said. "And this is a sign that no one must come into the village for fear they will bring sickness with them. Wait a moment while I call and find out." Then Ohn Bwint cupped his hands to his mouth and called, "Uncle, Uncle." Almost at once an old man put his head out of his house.

"Is there sickness over the hills, Uncle?" Ohn Bwint asked.

"Yes. Four people died at Lerdo-Ki, and the village has moved two miles farther along the trail," he replied fearfully.

We gathered together and had a little council of war. Six tigers and four deaths from sickness, and the village has moved! Should we return to Awbawa, and then go back by train and boat? Or should we go forward? We were halfway across the hills. Three or four more days, and we would be home again. What should we do?

"God is with us. Let us go forward!" Ohn Bwint said. "Yes! Yes! Forward, forward!" the boys chorused, and off we went with Ohn Bwint taking the lead.

Up, up, up we went. Then down, down, down. We found the old deserted village of Lerdo-Ki, but it was evening before we found the new village. The boys were tired and exhausted, but we had a good meeting there, and the next day we arrived at the little town of Papun, the district government headquarters.

We rested that night at the Baptist mission, and the next morning we marched down the streets playing the band and "Ingathering" in every house and shop on the street. There was an offering large or small from every home, and since there was a dirt road from this town to our mission station fifty miles away, we hired a motor bus for the last stretch of our journey home.

"They're back. They're back," shouted the boys who had stayed behind to look after the mission. And covered with dust, the happy boys unloaded their instruments and other baggage.

"How did you like the . . . ?"

"Are you glad to get back?"

"Did you see . . . ?" The questions were fired at us.

"Oh, say, there's a letter for Maung Thein," said San Yok, our mission overseer, all of a sudden. "Here, Maung Thein."

Trembling with excitement and weariness, Maung Thein took the letter and read out loud:

"On the fourth day of the month of May your aunt is to be married.

Come and help us with the wedding.

Signed, Your Father."

The
Earthquake

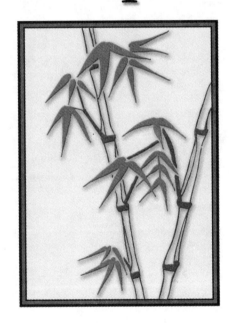

Chapter 10

"Shall I go, Thara? Shall I go?" Maung Thein asked excitedly.

"Go. Go by all means, my lad, and God go with you," I replied. "Maybe this is the answer to our prayers."

So early the next morning, after cleaning up and after a good night's rest, Maung Thein started off on the trail so very familiar to him, the trail to his own home, to his mother and to his father.

"Maung Thein's come! It's Maung Thein!" his father shouted excitedly as the dusty, weary boy climbed up the ladder into his home, and in a few moments everybody was there—his mother, his brothers, his sisters, and a great company of village folks.

"I saw you on the boat," his mother said while her eyes glistened with tears.

"And I saw you—and Aung Thein and Aung Twe," Maung Thein said. Then for the next two or three days he told of the wonderful trip to Rangoon city. He told of the boat ride, the train ride, the meeting for the white people in the city. He told of fire carts and thunder carts, and animals and great big boats. He told of the Awbawa camp meeting, of the march back home over the hills, and of the six tigers we never saw. The other mothers in the village looked enviously at Maung Thein's mother and said, "We wish our sons played in the brass band."

And now listen!

The fourth of May came, the guests for the wedding came, and the preparations for the feast were all made. On that very night, at eight-thirty, while the wedding festivities were going on, Burma was shaken with the greatest earthquake yet known in that district. The city of Pegu, a hundred miles across the valleys, was almost blotted out, and two thousand dead lay buried in its crumbled ruins. Our mission station rocked to and fro, but our buildings being of wood, no serious damage came to us. The house with the wedding guests in it also rocked to and fro, and in a moment faces whitened, eyes protruded, and knees knocked together as screaming voices called out, "What's the matter? What's the matter?"

Maung Thein sprang to his feet. "Don't be frightened," he commanded. "Don't be frightened. It's an earthquake. We learned all about earthquakes up at the school."

"An earthquake? And you know all about earthquakes?" his father said. "Good, good! My son knows all about earthquakes. But first let us go to the pagoda and ask the Buddhist priest, for my son is but a lad. Let us hear the words of the old man first."

But they found the Buddhist priest beside his broken pagoda as frightened as anyone else. "Earthquakes?" he said. "Who knows? Maybe it is the evil one, maybe the spirits, but I don't know."

"Then we will ask the witch," his father said. "She talks with spirits, and maybe she can tell." But they found the witch trembling with hysterics as she lay on her mat. "Isn't it awful. Isn't it awful!" was all that she could say.

"Well, that's strange," Maung Thein's father said. "The priest doesn't know, and the witch doesn't know, but my son knows. Here, Maung Thein, stand up here and tell these people all about the earthquake." And with the Word of God in his hand and the courage of God in his heart, Maung Thein preached the signs of Christ's second coming till after midnight. He told of the earth growing old. He told of the warning message to get ready as found in the Bible and in the tracts he had given to all who could read. He told of the message of the brass band as it went around the jungle telling people to get ready. And now he said, "God is using the voice of the earthquake so that all may know."

"He's right. He's right," the old men agreed. "The lad speaks truly." And one by one, their fears allayed, they went off to their houses to sleep. One by one, they went away till there was only one person left, and it was Maung Thein's mother!

"Maung Thein, my son, Mother is so proud of you," she said. "Mother doesn't like to see you leaving the house. Tomorrow morning you will be going back to school, so tonight Mother is going to sleep in her brother's house. And in the morning you get up early and cook your rice; then as the sun is coming up on the horizon, you start back to school. And Mother won't have to see you going away."

With these words her voice choked, and she began to sob. Maung Thein went up into his house, and spread his mat on the floor. He lay down, but not to sleep. His heart was too full. God had answered his prayers. God had changed the hearts of his parents. God was with him, and burying his face in his hands, he sobbed out his praise to God. Then he lay down and just counted his blessings over and over. Everybody had been so good— Thara Pa Do and Thara Peter and Perfume. Perfume had prayed for him, too. Perfume had told him never to give up. Wouldn't she be glad to hear the good news when she came back with Ma Ma from the hill station, when the new school year began. Would she . . . ?

"We Want a Teacher"

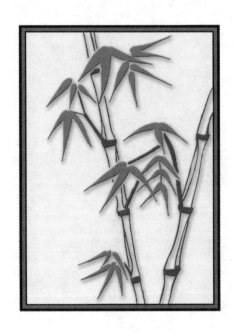

Chapter 11

In a few days, the students began to come back for the new school year. And one evening the motor launch was to go down to Shwegon to meet the river steamer to bring Ma Ma Hare and the children and the school supplies back from the hill station and the city.

"Maung Thein, would you like to come down to Shwegon with me and San Yok and help with the luggage?" I said as I passed the boys' dorm when the students were eating their afternoon meal.

"I would love to go," Maung Thein said. I thought I caught a hint of extra gladness in his voice, but of course everybody loved Ma Ma and wanted to see her come back. In about two hours we were at Shwegon, and before long the river steamer arrived. There were Lenny and Eileen waving. There was Ma Ma, and beside her was Perfume. "Oh, ho," I said to myself, "so that's why Maung Thein is so glad to see Ma Ma again!"

We tied up along side of the steamer and for a few moments were busy with our greetings. "We've heard all about it," Perfume said breathlessly.

"About Mother coming to the riverside to see me?" Maung Thein asked.

"Yes, and about the band at Rangoon and the earthquake," Perfume added.

"And about the old witch and the Buddhist priest?"

"Yes, I'm so, . . . *we're* so happy."

"I'll tell you all about it going up the river," Maung Thein said. "We've got to get loaded now."

And never were sacks and bundles so light before. And never were the three long hours upriver to the mission station so short before. San Yok steered the launch skillfully. Ma Ma and I reviewed all the doings of the children while they had been away, and Maung Thein told Perfume all about his experiences.

"I knew He would," Perfume said so all of us could hear.

"I knew God would soften their hearts if you'd just be true and faithful. And you were! I knew you would. I am so proud of you."

It was midnight by the time we were all unloaded, but everybody was happy, and that was the beginning of a good year for Maung Thein. It was his last year at Kamamaung School. If all went well, he would go to the Meiktila Training School the next year. But he had to work all of his way. Although his parents' attitude had changed and their anger had lessened, to save face his father still refused to help with any school fees. But still, it was a good year.

The next summer vacation came and went. School was about to open again, and Maung Thein was counting his cash to see how he would come out with train fare and tuition, when suddenly he didn't feel well. He had a sore throat, a runny nose, and a fever. Maung Thein was down with the measles!

"Measles! Never mind, Maung Thein," I said. "We'll move you into the hospital, and we'll look after you like a king, and you'll soon be better."

But Maung Thein had a hard time. For a few days even the dainties that Ma Ma sent over to him by the hand of Perfume failed to tempt his appetite.

"I'm afraid I can't go to Meiktila, Thara," he said sadly. "It will be too late by the time I am able to travel."

"Never mind, Maung Thein," I comforted. "Just rest and get better. Remember, God is still with you." And it was then that a delegation of village elders came one day from Tiger Village two miles away on the other side of the river.

"Thara, we're ready for our village school now," they said.

"You are?" I asked in surprise.

"Yes, we're ready now."

"But only two years ago you said that if we started a school in your village you would burn it down!"

"We know, Thara, we know. But for two years we have looked at Kamamaung School. For two years we have seen your teachers come and go, and they are true men. Where they teach, light shines in the darkness. The sick get better, and people are not afraid anymore. We cannot wait any longer. We want a school now."

"But I have no money to build a school now," I replied.

"We have built the school already," they said.

"But my money is all planned for this year. I could not pay a teacher," I replied. "Maybe I'll try to do something for you next year."

"Never mind the money, Thara. Give us a teacher. We will feed him and give him a basket of rice for each student."

"Do you think you could get a man to teach for wages as small as that?" I asked hopelessly. And just then I heard someone calling from the hospital ward. "Thara, Thara. Please won't you let me go? I did hope to go to Meiktila Training School this year, but I can't make it now. Thara, can't I go to Tiger Village and be the teacher?"

It was Maung Thein!

Very
Tall

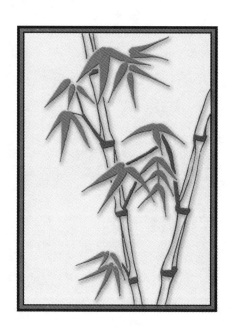

Chapter 12

B ut, Maung Thein, did you hear the wages they will pay?"

"Never mind the wages, Thara. Maybe I can win some souls in Tiger Village. That's the wages I want," he replied earnestly.

So Maung Thein went to Tiger Village, and about twenty-two boys and girls came to his little school there. Among these little heathen children was a ten-year-old boy named Very Tall. Now jungle mothers give character names to their children, and this little fellow must have been a very long baby when he was born. His mother really should have called him Longfellow, but she was thinking of him standing up, so she called him Very Tall. This little lad lived in a village four miles away. But in order that he could come to school he was staying with an uncle in Tiger Village. He had been at school only a few weeks when he saw something yellow that shone like gold in his teacher's Bible.

"What's that, Thara?" he asked.

"Why, that's a Sabbath School bookmark," Maung Thein said, "and everybody who studies his Sabbath

School lesson every day and goes to Sabbath School every week for a year gets a beautiful golden ribbon like this one."

"Do they?" Very Tall said, his eyes widening with wonder. "And if I study my Sabbath School lesson every day and go to Sabbath School every week for a year, can I get one, too?"

"You certainly can."

"Then that's what I'm going to do," he said. "I want a golden ribbon that shines like the golden streets of the New Jerusalem." And he started in earnest. At the end of the first quarter he received a perfect record card. At the end of the second quarter he received another. At the end of the third quarter he received another. Then he started to count the Sabbaths that remained until he would complete one whole year.

"Only five more Sabbaths. Only four more Sabbaths. Only three . . ." And then one day an old man came from Very Tall's village. He walked into the school house, sat down, and spread apart the bamboos in the floor enough to spit out his wad of betel nut. Then leaning over, he touched Very Tall on the shoulder and said, "Very Tall, your mother's very sick. You have to go home and eat the devil worship so she can get better again." And Very Tall was very sad all the rest of the afternoon. Long after the other children had left the school, he sat there wondering what he could do. He loved his mother, and he loved going home. It wasn't that that made him sad. But how could he keep up his perfect Sabbath School record in his village? There wasn't a Bible in the whole village. There was nobody who could read, and there wasn't a single Christian, and the devil worship might take two weeks. It might take three. And there were only three more Sabbaths between him and his golden book mark.

Suddenly an idea struck him. He jumped down the school ladder, ran down the trail through the mango trees, and raced up the ladder to his teacher's room. "Thara," he panted, "Thara, I've just thought, haven't you got two Bibles? And couldn't you lend me one? I'd be so careful with it. I really would. And Thara, then I could keep up my record; I could have Sabbath School all by myself. Please, Thara."

"Of course you may have my extra Bible, Very Tall," Maung Thein said, and turning down the pages where that week's lesson and the next week's lesson were, he handed it to Very Tall.

"Thank you, Thara. Thank you, Thara," Very Tall said. And putting his teacher's Bible carefully under his little coat right next to his little heart, he waved goodbye, climbed down the ladder, and disappeared down the trail through the jungle bamboos calling out, "I'll be faithful, Thara! I'll be faithful!"

Maung Thein's heart beat with joy as he saw the little fellow go, and he stood there for a moment realizing that there is no joy on earth that can compare to the joy of seeing others coming out of darkness into light because of something you have done.

Then he realized that it was time to cook his evening meal. He turned around, lit a fire, and put on a pot of rice to cook. Then he reached into the basket that hung on the wall to get some vegetables to put in the stew. The basket was empty, but that didn't matter. There were plenty of things in the jungle to eat. All he had to do was to go get them. So swinging his basket onto his back, he took down the big knife that hung on the wall and set off down the same trail that Very Tall had taken a little while before.

Maung Thein was not going anywhere in particular. He was not walking quickly. He was looking for roots and leaves and bamboo shoots, and he walked slowly, turning now to the left, and now to the right, to pick some leaves or dig a root. So you can imagine his surprise when, after walking only a few hundred yards, he came to a small clearing in the bamboos and found Very Tall sitting right there under a tree. Very Tall saw his teacher at the same moment and quickly smuggled something under the corner of his jacket. Then he hung his head as if in shame, and his ears went fiery red. Maung Thein was so shocked he couldn't think of what to say. But Very Tall slowly stood up and came toward him.

Why that look of guilt? Maung Thein thought. *Why those red ears? Whatever has Very Tall been doing?*

The Devil
Worship

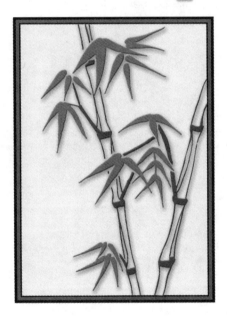

Chapter 13

The only thing that Maung Thein could think as he saw Very Tall coming toward him with such a downcast, guilty look was that he had been smoking or chewing betel nut. Just at the end of the village there was a spirit altar at the foot of a big spirit tree, and on that altar there was a generous supply of tobacco and betel nut that passersby had placed there to bring them good luck. *Was the temptation too much for you, Very Tall?* Maung Thein thought.

By this time, however, Very Tall was close enough to speak, and with his head still hanging apparently in shame, he said in a loud, hoarse whisper, "Thara, Thara, will God be angry with me for . . . for . . . reading the Bible in the jungle?"

"For what?" Maung Thein gasped.

"For reading the Bible in the jungle."

"Oh, Very Tall! Is that what you've been doing? I thought, . . . I thought when I saw your red face and your red ears that when you passed the spirit altar and saw the betel nut and tobacco, that the temptation had been too strong for you and you had been chewing . . ."

"What! Me? Me chew betel nut? Oh no, Thara! I wouldn't touch the dirty stuff. I haven't touched it ever since I came to school. But Thara, I began to think that if I came to a hard word in the Bible that I couldn't read, and since in my village there is no one who can read, and since it's too far to come and ask you—so I thought, . . . I thought I had better try reading my Sabbath School lessons before I went home. And I can, Thara! I can read every word. But tell me, . . . tell me, . . . will God be angry with me for reading the Bible in the jungle?"

"No, no, my boy. God won't be angry with you," Maung Thein assured him, patting him on the back. "God loves for us to read the Bible everywhere—in the school, in the house, in the field, or in the jungle."

"Ah, well, then," Very Tall said, smiling with relief as he took the Bible from under the corner of his jacket and put it again near to his heart. "You needn't worry about me chewing dirty old betel nut or tobacco. I'll be faithful, Thara. I'll be faithful." And waving goodbye, he disappeared down the trail through the bamboos of the jungle.

Before long he was clambering up the bamboo ladder into his own bamboo house. His poor sick mother was lying on a mat near the fire. She heard someone coming and raised her head. Seeing it was Very Tall, she called to him in a weak, sickly voice, "Very Tall, I see you've come. Go and tell your father that you're here, and tell him to roast the pig. Then tonight, when everybody is asleep, we will sacrifice to the devils."

Obediently Very Tall ran and found his father and gave him his mother's message. That night, after everybody had gone to sleep, the father gathered his little family around the roast pig in the dim light of one little oil lamp, and holding hands and swaying their bodies, they prayed something like this:

"Oh devils, oh devils,

here's a pig for you. Here's a pig for you.

Don't be angry with us. Don't be angry with us.

Let Mother get better. Let Mother get better.

Oh devils, oh devils."

They prayed, and they prayed. Then they waited, and they waited. They waited for three days, but the mother didn't get better. And the poor sick woman said, "Husband, I don't think the devils liked the pig. I think the devils want a chicken."

So they went through the sacrifice all over again, and they prayed, and they prayed. Then they waited, and they waited. They waited three more days. Then the poor sick woman said, "Husband, I think I'm going to die. I've eaten the root medicine and the leaf medicine and the bark medicine. I've had the devil doctor bewitch me, and now we've given the devils a pig and a chicken; but I feel worse than I ever did."

"Mother, Mother, there's one more thing we can do. Two miles away the golden Buddhist priest sits in his golden robe beside his golden pagoda. I'll send for him and have him come and say his golden prayers. And then maybe you'll get better."

Early the next morning, heralded by two big boys who

banged a big brass gong that hung from a bamboo pole carried on their shoulders, the Buddhist priest came slowly into the village. As the gong sounded, the village folk came running to the trail along which the priest would walk, and as the priest went along, they all knelt down and bowed with their hands and foreheads touching the ground.

Did I say *everybody* bowed down? I should have said, "everybody but Very Tall," for Very Tall stood straight and very tall and did not bow one inch. He didn't call himself a Christian yet. But he was a Sabbath School member, and he had learned in the mission school in Tiger Village not to worship anything but the living God, who made heaven and earth and everything. So while the others all bowed down, Very Tall stood up straight. And his poor, sick mother, lying on her mat, saw him standing straight and tall, and it made her very angry. The straighter he stood, the more angry she became till at last she could not keep in her hot, bitter words, but screamed out with all the strength she had left, "Bow down, you little white-toothed dog! Bow down, you little white-toothed dog! Can't you see that the priest has come to pray for me? Bow down, you little white-toothed dog!"

Then Very Tall Prayed

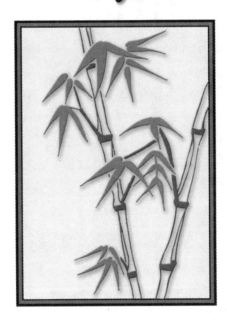

Chapter 14

Poor little Very Tall! I knew how he felt that day. I've been called a white-toothed dog, and it doesn't make you feel very happy. Very Tall looked at his mother, and he looked at the priest. He didn't want to be disobedient, and he didn't want to be disrespectful. But while he was wondering what to do, his father ran up the bamboo ladder and went over to his wife and whispered, "Mother, don't make Very Tall worship the priest. You know nothing has made you better yet, and I've been thinking, . . . I've been thinking maybe even the priest's prayers won't make you better. And then, Mother, maybe Very Tall knows how to pray to the white man's God, and then maybe you will get better."

So Very Tall didn't have to worship the priest; he just stood there watching the priest as he slowly went up the ladder and seated himself behind a big palm leaf fan. Then the two boys who carried the brass gong lit small candles and put them in a circle all around the sick mother. Then the priest rang his little golden bell and said his golden prayers. And he prayed, and he prayed, and he prayed, and he prayed—but the poor sick mother didn't get better.

"Now I just know that I'm going to die," the mother said after they had waited three days. "I just feel worse than ever."

But the father said, "Mother, don't give up yet. Let me ask Very Tall if he can pray." Then the father called, "Very Tall! Oh, Very Tall!" And as Very Tall came running up the ladder, Father said, "Very Tall, do they teach you to pray to the white man's God down there at the mission school in Tiger Village?"

"Oh yes, Father, and I can pray a little bit."

"Well, you know nothing has seemed to make Mother better. We've tried all the village medicine; we've tried the devil worship; even the golden priest's prayers don't do any good. I've been wondering if you could pray to the white man's God."

"Oh yes, Father. I can. And Father, we don't have to wait to pray until night when everyone has gone to bed. And we don't have to light any candles or ring any gongs. Yes, Father, we can do it. I'll show you how. Get the children, Father."

"All right, all right."

"Father, all you've got to do is to kneel down and put your hands together and shut your eyes. And when I'm finished, you say, 'Amen,' and then God will make Mother better. I know He will, Father."

So that is what they did. They gathered together on their knees around the wondering sick woman, and then Very Tall prayed.

"Please, Jesus, make Mother better.

"Mother and Father don't know You yet.

"But they have tried everything they know to make Mother better.

"Please, Jesus, if You would make her well, then they would know that You are the biggest, kindest God and stronger than all their evil spirits.

"Please, Jesus, make Mother better.

"In Your name, Amen."

And I think our living God must have sent some very happy angels to answer that little prayer at once.

The father had to swallow hard before he could say, "Amen." And the mother put out her thin, weak arm and drew Very Tall close to her. As her little boy prayed, her heart was moved as it had never been moved before. The tears rolled down her face as she said, "How could you do it? How could you do it, Very Tall, when I cursed you so bitterly and called you a white-toothed dog? How could you do it? But Very Tall, Mother is feeling better already; she is. I think Mother will be all better soon."

And she was! The very next morning she could sit up, and the next day she could stand up. And the next day she threw her arms around her little boy and said, "Very Tall, you must go back to school. Your lessons must not stop for too long. But when you get back, tell your teacher that it wasn't the devil worship that made Mother better, and it wasn't the priest's prayers that made Mother better; but it was her own little boy's prayers to the living God that made Mother better."

Very Tall took up his precious Bible and put it under his jacket near to his little heart. Then he said Goodbye to his father and his mother and his brothers and his sisters and bounded down the bamboo ladder and raced as fast as his legs would carry him along the trail through the bamboos and over the little hills back to Tiger Village.

Then running up the bamboo ladder to his teacher's room, puffing and panting, he said, "Please, teacher, thank you so much for lending me your Bible. Be sure to mark me up with two big sevens on the class record card, because I studied my lesson three times every day, and on the two Sabbaths I had Sabbath School all day long.

"Oh, Mother says to tell you she is all better again, but it wasn't the devil worship that made her better, and it wasn't the priest's prayers that made her better, but when I prayed to the living God, then she got better. Thara, be sure to mark me up with two big sevens, won't you?"

Of course, Maung Thein did, and in a few weeks it was my pleasure to present Very Tall with the beautiful yellow ribbon that shone like the golden streets of the New Jerusalem.

Very Tall was very happy. But he was not the happiest person in Tiger Village that day. Maung Thein's heart was full of joy, and he found it hard to keep back the tears. Suddenly he wanted to tell someone, someone whom he was sure would understand.

Perfume Said "Yes"

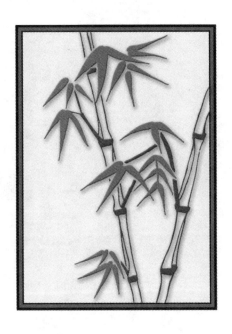

Chapter 15

I'll be coming down to the mission station tomorrow," Maung Thein said as I said Goodbye after the Sabbath service in which I had presented Very Tall with his golden Sabbath School bookmark.

"We will be looking for you," I said cheerfully, with maybe a little emphasis on the *we*. It was customary for all of my "remote" school teachers to come to the main station on the first Sunday of each new quarter and bring their reports. We had a workers' meeting, and it was inspiring to hear the news from the various stations. But since Maung Thein was only two miles and one big river away, he frequently came to the main station on Sundays for supplies and medicines, and he generally had dinner with Thara Peter, our head evangelist.

"I think that's Maung Thein calling on the other side of the river," Perfume said on Sunday morning as we finished family worship.

"Fine," I said, "we'll have San Yok go over in the launch to bring him across. But say, Perfume, how did you know it was Maung Thein?"

"Oh, I just knew," she said with a trace of a blush.

It *was* Maung Thein. He had brought a few of the village folk with him who wanted some medicine, so I took them to the dispensary, leaving Maung Thein to talk with Ma Ma and Perfume.

"Did you hear about Very Tall's golden ribbon?" he asked.

"We surely did! And you must have been very happy about it, too," Ma Ma said.

"I was," Maung Thein said. "I never thought there could be such joy in all the world. Did you hear about the children having Sabbath School during the half-yearly holidays?"

"No."

"Well, when I left to spend a few days at home, I told them to be faithful, and they said they would. But on Sabbath, when they came to have Sabbath School, they found some travelers resting in the school house. One of them was a Buddhist priest. For a moment they didn't know what to do. Then one of them said, 'Aye, I know what to do. Let's go down to the banana garden and have Sabbath School there.'

" 'Sure,' agreed the others. 'Didn't Jesus and His disciples have Sabbath School in the garden and on the mountains?' So off they went to the banana garden, and there they sang 'Jesus Loves Me' and 'When He Cometh, When He Cometh,' and they had Sabbath School all by themselves!"

"And that made you happy, too."

"It surely did. I just love those children, and I love my work so much."

"Maung Thein," Perfume said, "you are a real missionary, just like Ma Ma and Thara Pa Do. I think it must be wonderful to be a real missionary. I would like to be a missionary like that, too." They talked pleasantly for a while, and then Maung Thein got a few supplies and went over to Thara Peter's place for dinner.

"Thara Peter," Maung Thein said a little nervously, when a lull in the conversation came.

"Yes, Maung Thein, what is it?"

"Oh nothing. Only I was just thinking . . ."

"Thinking what?"

"Oh, just about my work."

"Yes, yes, your work, and . . . ?"

"And you know I like my work so much. But, it takes me so much time to do my cooking."

"Quite so," Thara Peter agreed, "and also it is hard doing all the singing all by yourself. Someone to help in the singing would be . . ."

"Why Thara Peter, how did you know I was thinking just that?"

"Do you forget that I was a young man not too long ago? And, of course, you know that you are on the Mission budget next school year. But tell me who is the young lady of your choice?"

"I wouldn't dare mention her name. But if you asked Ma Ma Hare, I think she could tell you."

"I think there is no need for me to ask Ma Ma Hare. Go back to your school, and come again next Sunday. Maybe I will have an answer for you then."

Maung Thein crossed the river and went back to Tiger Village with a heart as light as a feather. And that evening Thara Peter and Ma Keh, his good wife, invited Perfume to dinner. It was a happy occasion. For they were all such good friends, but after the children had gone out to play and while Ma Keh was washing the dishes, Thara Peter lowered his voice to a whisper and said, "Perfume, there was a young man visiting with me today. He is a real missionary, a real soul winner. We know him well. He is doing a good job with his school. But he finds that it takes so much time to cook, and he needs someone to help in the singing."

"And who does he want?" Perfume asked in a glow of excitement that could not be hidden.

"He didn't say the name."

"He didn't?" There was just a shade of disappointment.

"No, but I know from other things he said that he means you."

"Me? Oh, Thara Peter, what a surprise! Are you sure he meant me?"

"Quite sure."

"I wonder what gave you the idea that he meant me!"

"You know, Thara Pa Do and Ma Ma are going on furlough next year, and they can't take you to America with them."

"No."

"So what shall I tell Maung Thein?"

"Oh, no! What about his parents and my parents?"

"I will talk to them both, but first I need to know if you are willing. You don't want to remain single all your life do you?"

"Oh, no!"

"You couldn't find a better, more faithful, more courageous young man in all the world, could you?"

"Oh, no."

"Then?"

There was a long, long pause during which the blood rushed unchecked into her cheeks. She lifted her eyes and whispered, "All right, tell him 'Yes.' " And with her heart pounding with delight, Perfume jumped up and ran as fast as her legs would carry her back to her room.

Glad Ending to
My Story

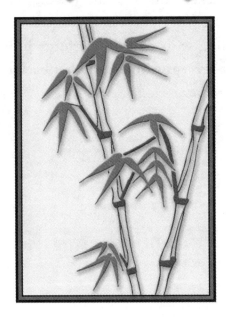

Chapter 16

As soon as possible, Thara Peter went to visit Maung Thein's parents and Perfume's parents, for this is the proper way to form engagements in the land of golden pagodas. He soon returned with the happy approval of all, and the wedding was set to take place at the beginning of the new school year.

May 18, 1933, was a day they would long remember. While Perfume had been with Ma Ma Hare during the summer vacation in the hill station, they had been sewing lovely dresses and other things for the new home. Maung Thein had been repairing the school house in Naung Karing, the new mission to which he had been assigned, and planting a garden near the house where they were to live.

The early rains had fallen, the mangoes were getting ripe, and the lawns were nice and green. Now the students were all back at school, and a nice mission wedding was all that was needed to make everybody happy.

Great pots of rice had been cooked, and great pots of stew prepared to eat with the rice, and long tables had

been placed on the lawn beside the mission house. For in
the East a wedding feast is still the most important part
of a wedding, and even passersby are invited to take part.
A group had come from Tiger Village. Very Tall and his
friends were there. Maung Thein's parents came up, and
all was ready.

At last the brass band began to play. The guests and
visitors all assembled in the chapel. The school choir
sang. Maung Thein and his best man stood with me at
the front of the chapel, and Perfume came in on Thara
Peter's arm. It was lovely! The service was just like one of
our American services, and everybody listened intently
to hear the bride and bridegroom say, "I do." I pro-
nounced them man and wife and introduced them to
the congregation. Then the choir sang as we marched
out and went over to the tables. Very soon we were all
sitting down to the feast. Perfume was a little shy, but
her blushing cheeks only made her more beautiful.

A score of dainty little girls saw that everyone was
served with a plate of rice and stew, and mangoes and
bananas were placed on the tables before us. Then came
the wedding cake for the important people and hundreds
of little cupcakes, one each, for everybody else.

I sat beside Maung Thein and Perfume, and in between the happy conversation I said, "David must have
seen young people disowned too, I think, or maybe he
was referring to Saul persecuting him, but he said, 'When
my father and my mother forsake me, then the Lord will
take me up.' It's true, isn't it?"

"It surely is true," Maung Thein agreed.

"And the Lord Jesus Himself promised, 'Every one of you that forsakes houses or brethren or sisters or father or mother or wife or children or lands for My name's sake, shall receive a hundredfold and shall inherit everlasting life.' And that's true, isn't it? Look, here are just a few of your brothers and sisters and fathers and mothers, and there are more than a hundred right here!"

"Yes, indeed, it's true, Thara," Maung Thein replied. "The Lord is so good. He works it all out in His own wonderful way."

Perfume tried to speak too, but she was too happy. The words wouldn't come. So she just nodded and looked more beautiful than ever.

• • •

Of course, this isn't really the end of the story. There will be no real end as long as Maung Thein and Perfume live and serve God. But they went to Naung Karing and were there for two years. Then, as the needs of the work and the conditions of war demanded, they filled post after post in the Tenasserim District until they were asked to be in charge of our mission in Balugyun, a big island at the mouth of the Salween River near Moulmein. In the last letter I received from Maung Thein he told me that God had blessed Perfume and him with three sons and two daughters. The oldest son is working at our Rangoon hospital, and the oldest daughter is taking the nurse's course. The three younger ones are all in school, preparing for work in the Lord's cause. But the best news of all was that Maung Thein had baptized fifteen people this year!

If you enjoyed this book, you can enjoy more Eric B. Hare stories on CD!

Classic Eric B. Hare Stories on CD! Three volumes

Favorite stories told by the master storyteller himself, in that well-remembered voice that makes little children's eyes get big and round! Includes lots of old favorites, such as "Mister Crooked Ears," "Pip, Pip the Naughty Chicken," and many more that older folks will remember. Three CDs to choose from—but you'll want all three.

Volume 1: Eight stories, including "Me Me," "Chinese Lady and the Rats," and "Mister Crooked Ears." 4-3330-0344-1. US$9.98.

Volume 2: Four stories: "The Hermit and the King," "White Bean," "Sweet Potatoes," and "Jack's Quarter." 4-3330-0344-2. US$9.98.

Volume 3: Seven stories, including "Who Put the Fire Out?" "The Mean Old Mistress," and "Impossible Fish Story." 4-3330-0344-3. US$9.98.

If you enjoy mission stories, you'll want to read more! Here's one you'll like.

Intrepid Gringo
Rosalie Mellor

Into the dark jungles where sunlight could not reach, Ross Sype brought the light of the gospel. In the face of malaria, superstition, and political unrest, he and his wife, Gertrude, shared the message of God in isolated mountain villages and on remote islands of Latin America. Paperback. 0-8163-2107-8. US$13.99.

Order from your ABC by calling **1-800-765-6955**, or get online and shop our virtual store at **http://www.AdventistBookCenter.com**.
- Read a chapter from your favorite book
- Order online
- Sign up for e-mail notices on new products

Prices subject to change without notice.